Dedicated to my brother, Yashky
who helps me find my things

First published in Great Britain in 2021
Independently published

Text and illustrations copyright © 2020 Ankara Prabdial
Concept by Ankara Prabdial in 2018
Illustrations by Ankara Prabdial and Yeimi Zárate

ISBN: 9798787472608

A Catalogue Record for this book is available from the British Library

THE SEA STOLE MY GLASSES

Ankara Prabdial   Yeimi Zárate

Little Ankara is tired.

Little Ankara is upset.

That morning, on the very first day of her holiday, she'd been splishing and splashing in the inky blue sea. Suddenly, a HUGE wave had crashed over her and swept her glasses out to sea!

Poor Ankara sits up in surprise. She searches for her glasses, but they are nowhere to be seen...

Now she just wants to go home.

Plop, bubble, bubble...
the glasses sink deeper into the inky blue sea.

Old Tommy Turtle is swimming nearby. He knocks into the pretty purple glasses and booms in his loud Scottish voice,

"Splishy Sploshy Splashes... I think I've found some glasses!"

The excited turtle puts them on and suddenly things are so much clearer.

He is so happy, he dances a merry jig.

Back in his driftwood hut, Tommy Turtle finds an old newspaper that he has wanted to read for ages.

He makes himself a mug of seaweed tea and with the radio humming in the background, he opens the wrinkled copy of the Undersea Times newspaper.

Ah, perfect!

He reads about how Flo Flounder got trapped in a bin bag, and how Chloe Clownfish had to be freed from a plastic bottle.

Oh dear!

Later that morning, Tommy Turtle goes to meet Olly Octopus.

When he sees his old friend, he cannot help but notice Olly looks a bit down.

Olly is grumpy because recently things are looking foggy. Tommy has a thought.

He takes the glasses off
and puts them on Olly.

Suddenly, Olly can see clearly.

What the octopus wants to see more than anything else are his beloved music sheets.

Olly turns to his piano and starts to play.

"Plinkety Plonkety Plank, I have my friend to thank!"

Outside, all the little octopi swim over and dance, swaying their tiny tentacles in time to the music. They have never heard such a wonderful melody before.

Olly hugs his friend tightly with his eight tentacles, thankful for letting him share the joy of music.

Even though Tommy cannot see as well anymore, it feels good to help his friend and make him smile.

Olly had made plans to have lunch at Winnie Whale's pink Tea Room at the bottom of the sea.

When he arrives, he tells her about the marvellous glasses that Tommy has given him.

Winnie is all a flutter because she has forgotten her recipe for her famous pearl cake.

She tells Olly that even though it is written down in Granny's recipe book, she cannot read Granny's squiggly writing without her spectacles. She thinks she had left them at M'n'S (Mussels and Shells) when she was there buying ingredients.

Olly knows he must help Winnie, and he knows how!

He will read the recipe and Winnie will follow it.

Together they begin to bake the cake.

Winnie pours out the last of the flour and in a massive white puff, her missing spectacles magically appear.

"Aaah aaah!" exclaims Winnie.

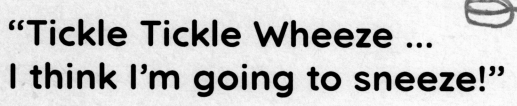

**"Tickle Tickle Wheeze ...
I think I'm going to sneeze!"**

Olly's eyes widen in panic as a
GINORMOUS blast of water erupts
from Winnie's blowhole.

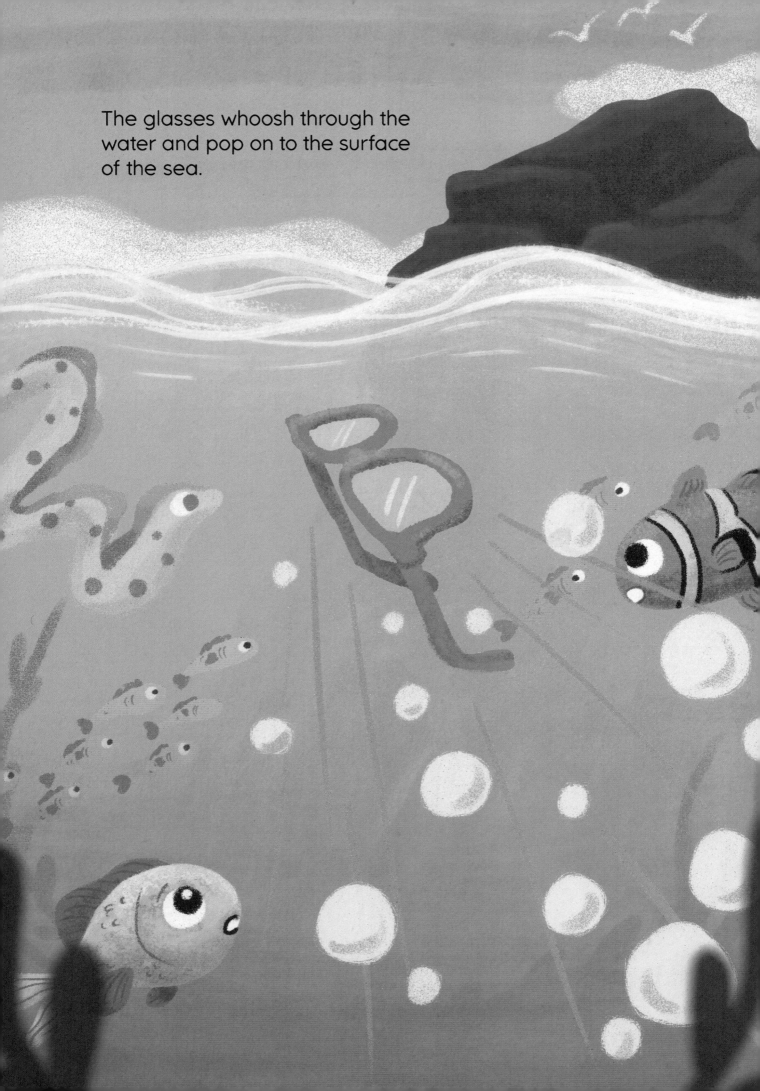

The glasses whoosh through the water and pop on to the surface of the sea.

Penelope Pelican is hovering nearby and she sees the shiny thing in the inky blue sea.

The chicks will love to play with this she thinks, as she pops the glasses on her head.

Flying back to the nest is difficult because Penelope is struggling to see clearly.

"Oh no!" Penelope snaps her bill together in fright, as a tall rock blurrily appears on her flight path.

With a last-minute swerve of her wing, she just manages to avoid disaster.

"Phew!" she breathes a sigh of relief.

But ... the glasses are not so lucky and fall into the depths of the inky blue sea with a silent **splash.**

Penelope dives and tries to find them but the sea swallows them up.

Young Danny Dolphin is practising holding his breath when a strange thing floats past him.

This looks like somebody's something he thinks, as he catches the glasses in his beak and makes his way to the surface of the sea.

Penelope has just about given up when Danny pops his head up and asks, "Dropped something?"

Penelope claps her wings together,
**"Hip Hip Hooray!
You've just saved the day!"**

Danny waves a fin goodbye to Penelope
and dives back into the inky blue sea.

Penelope tucks the glasses safely
into her bill and flies into the
crimson sunset on her
way home.

She soon reaches her messy clifftop nest and empties her bill.
A tin can, the glasses and shiny bits of plastic all tumble out.
The chicks begin to fight over the treasures.

Peering from her lofty clifftop, Penelope hears a sad voice down below.

She can see little Ankara down on the beach, telling her brother all about her lost glasses.

Selfish Penelope does not want Ankara to have the shiny thing.

Her chicks are more important to her.

Penelope smiles at her chicks, as they play peek-a-boo with all the treasures.

Penelope looks back on her day:

How lucky she was to have found the smelly tin can lodged in the rocks.

How she caught the plastic fish-like things bobbing in the waves.

How she saw the shiny glasses in the inky blue sea, and how Danny had rescued them for her.

She wonders what other adventures the glasses may have had earlier.

She watches Ankara closely.
The little girl is tired.
The little girl is upset.
The little girl just wants to go home.

Penelope can see clearly now that the little
girl needs them more than she does.

Penelope glides down and gently drops the glasses beside the girl, as she squawks,

"Caw Caw Cree...
You need them
more than me!"

Little Ankara picks the glasses up with sheer delight and puts them back on her smiling face.

She runs to her Mummy and Daddy and laughs,

"Can you see?
My glasses have come back to me!"

On the other side of the beach,
the sea steals little Yashky's hat...

Saving the Oceans from Plastic Waste:

Many people from around the world are still using plastic unnecessarily, as part of their everyday lives - it seems we cannot escape it. This stuff is everywhere - from your online purchase packaging ... to a simple pencil sharpener. Right now, you may be drinking from a disposable plastic bottle, not knowing that this same bottle could hurt or even kill a marine animal!

Well done to you if you have made the effort to source and use bioplastics; or even if you recycle your plastic waste. Sadly, most people still do not; according to 2021 statistics, the average amount of plastic rubbish each person in the UK produces is 99kg per year.

In a recent homework study regarding plastic in marine environments, I was horrified to learn that around 33% of all fish, including many consumed by humans, contain microplastics. Also, it is extremely worrying to have noted that a ten-year study completed in 2020 showed that the proportion of fish consuming microplastics, doubled across all species.

As of 2021, approximately one million sea birds die each year because of plastic waste, while the world's shoppers continue to use 500 billion single-use plastic bags per year.

Humans are now acknowledging the challenge of plastic in our seas and are beginning to protect the wildlife in our oceans from plastic waste with many clean-up projects being set up by non-profit organisations like WWF, Sea Shepherd, Sea Change Trust, The Ocean Clean Up, and many others.

Still, the problem lies with changing the mindset of the public – so, whether it is trash hunting or raising money for these causes, please do your part in saving these beautiful marine creatures and plants ...and our precious planet.

Printed in Great Britain
by Amazon